The Little Spotted Fish

for Jason

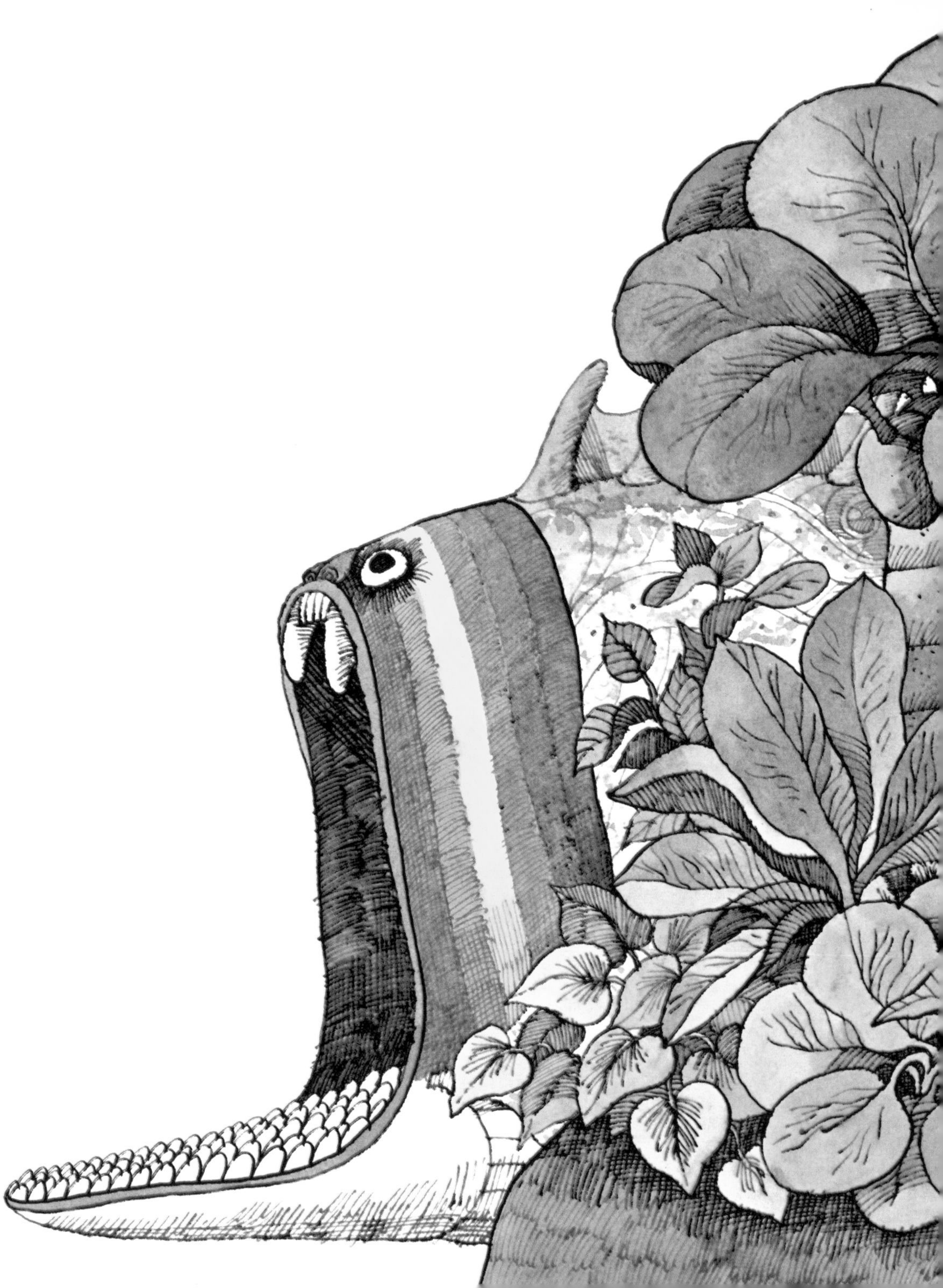

The Little Spotted Fish

by Jane Yolen

illustrated by Friso Henstra

A Clarion Book

THE SEABURY PRESS · NEW YORK

Library of Congress Cataloging in Publication Data

Yolen, Jane H.
    The little spotted fish.

    "A Clarion book."
    SUMMARY: Two times the little spotted fish saves
the fisherlad's life, but the third time the fish itself
is in danger.
    [1. Fairy tales]   I. Henstra, Friso, illus.
II. Title.
PZ8.Y78Li   [E]   74-14819
ISBN 0-8164-3134-5

The Little Spotted Fish

Once on a large island where the grass ran green to the sea, there lived a fisherlad all alone.

He fished the island's streams. He swam in its ponds. And when the thirst was upon him, he drank from the clear crystal springs.

And though other folk might have pitied him for his poor estate, he did not pity himself.

Now one day the fisherlad, whose name was Dylan, came upon a strange lake deep in a tangled wood. At the lake's edge, as if in wait for him, lay a coracle, as fine and fit a boat as he had ever seen. The hide was stretched tight over its wooden frame and it floated just within reach.

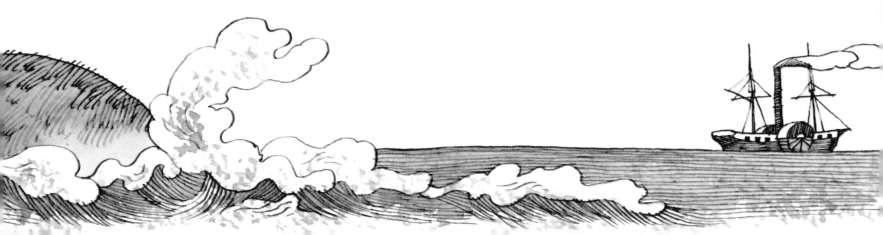

So Dylan climbed in and, to his surprise, the boat rowed itself far out into the middle of the lake before he could lay a hand to its paddle.

Suddenly, what should jump up in front of the boat but a little spotted fish.

As it leaped, it spouted water from its mouth. And as the water rained down before Dylan's eyes, he heard this song:

Dylan, Dylan, son of the wave,
The spotted fish thy life shall save.

"That is strange," thought Dylan as the fish disappeared beneath the water. For surely his life was not in danger. But knowing that magic was magic and should be carefully considered, he began to paddle ashore.

Dylan had but pulled a stroke or maybe two when he noticed a golden rod he had not seen before lying between his boots. He bent to pick up the pole and, as he did, there was a great thrashing in the water.

A monstrous fish arose in the lake. It had teeth as large as harpoons and a horrible growl issued from its throat.

Dylan felt his bones turn to water and he could do nought but stare. Finally, with an effort, he shook his head and shook off the fear and knew at once what to do.

He grabbed hold of the golden rod and threw it at the fish.

No sooner did the magic rod touch the fish than the fish flipped its mighty tail and disappeared into the deeps. The water was calm once more, the rod floating upon it like a feather in a pool.

"That is indeed strange," thought Dylan, who knew nothing about magic and all about fish. However, it was a beautiful rod, more beautiful than any Dylan had ever owned. So he rowed over to retrieve it, rowed ashore, went through the tangled wood and home.

For days Dylan fished with the magic golden rod, and fish sprang to his line in a shower of silver fins.

But at length Dylan grew tired of such easy catch, for it was not in him to use magic instead of skill.

So at last he walked himself through the tangled wood and found the lake once more.

There he laid the rod on the lake and said:

Little spotted fish, little spotted fish,
Take back the golden rod, that is Dylan's wish.

And before the water had time for a ripple, the rod had disappeared.

Dylan wondered about the magic rod for a day or two, for surely fishing without it was more difficult than fishing with. Then he thought about it no more. For there was much to do in living each day, and no time to worry about what was past.

A year and a day later, he chanced through the tangled wood once more and happened upon the same still lake. The coracle was waiting, its hide shimmering like the sea.

Again he climbed in, again the boat rowed itself, and again the little spotted fish jumped up in front of him. As it leaped, it spouted water from its mouth.

As the water rained down before Dylan's eyes, he heard this song:

> *Dylan, Dylan, son of the wave,*
> *The spotted fish thy life shall save.*

This time Dylan was prepared for danger, though none seemed near.

No sooner had he begun to row ashore than once again the waters of the lake trembled and shivered. And once again the monstrous fish rose out of the water with teeth like harpoons. Only this time a second rose behind it, bigger by half than the first, with whiskers taut as the rigging of a ship. And a horrible growling issued from the throats of the two.

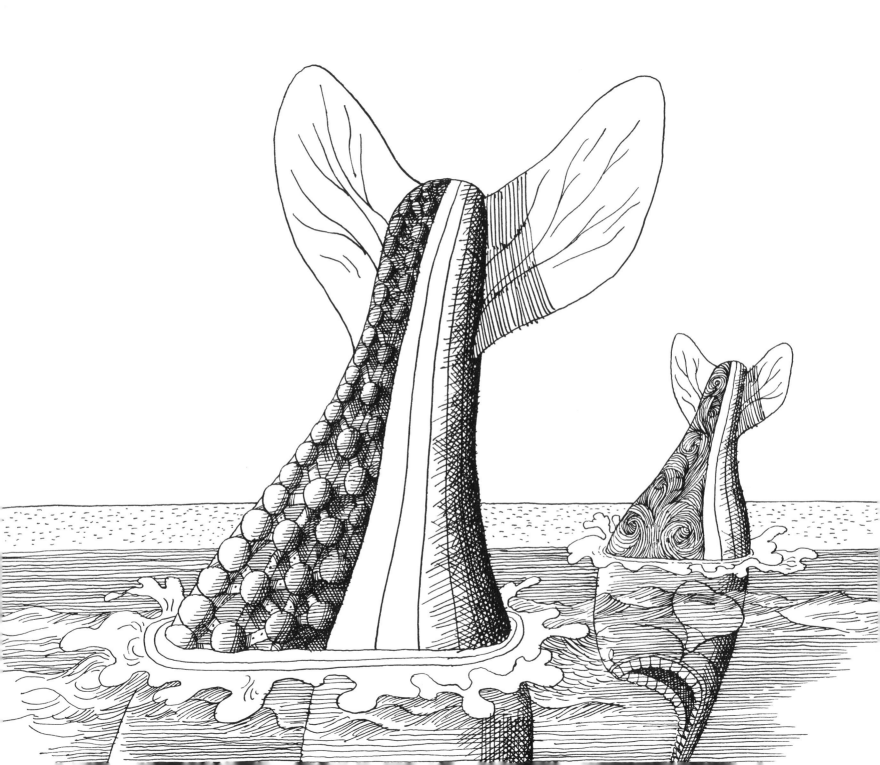

Dylan looked down at his feet, for he was expecting magic help. And help there was. A golden net lay between his boots. He picked up the net and heaved it at the two. No sooner did the magic net touch them than the fish flipped their mighty tails and disappeared into the lake. Then the waters were calm once more.

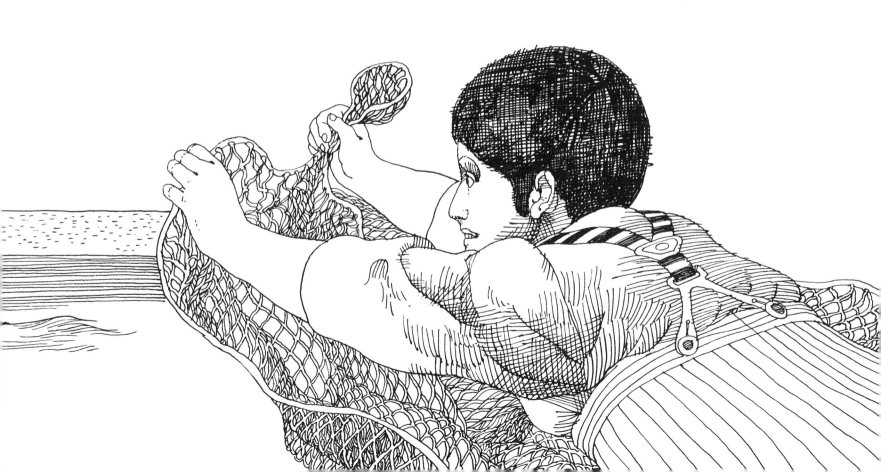

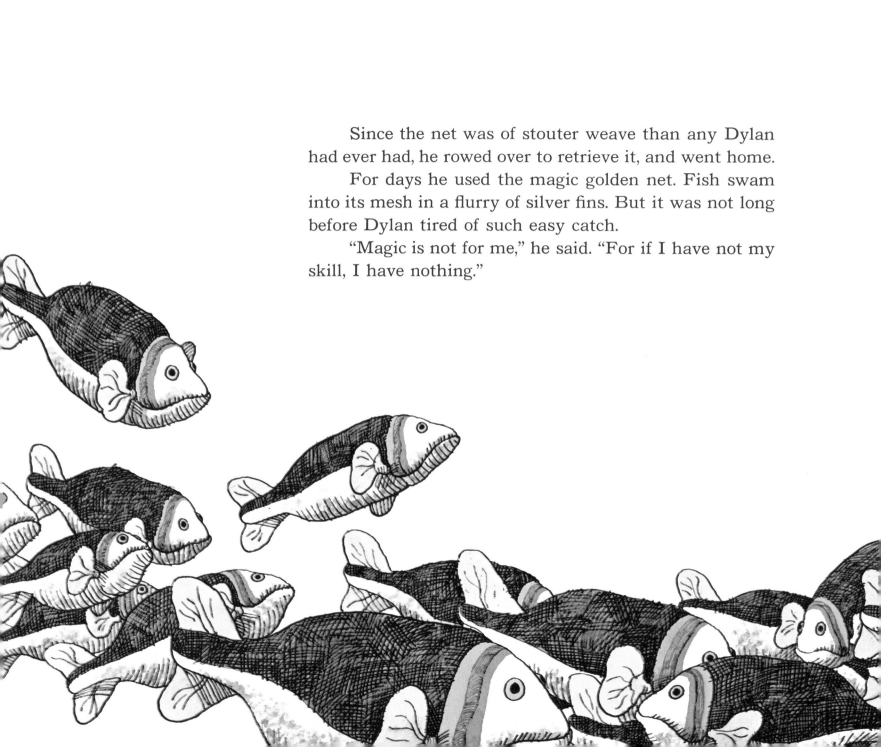

Since the net was of stouter weave than any Dylan had ever had, he rowed over to retrieve it, and went home.

For days he used the magic golden net. Fish swam into its mesh in a flurry of silver fins. But it was not long before Dylan tired of such easy catch.

"Magic is not for me," he said. "For if I have not my skill, I have nothing."

So he walked back to the lake in the middle of the tangled wood and threw in the net as far as he could, saying:

Little spotted fish, little spotted fish,
Take back the golden net, that is Dylan's wish.

Before the water had time to ripple, the net had disappeared.

A year and a day later, Dylan chanced in the wood again, and as before he climbed into the same small coracle in the same lake.

As before, the little spotted fish jumped up in front of him. And as it leaped, water spouted from its mouth. But this time the water was as red as blood, and the words the fish sang were different:

Dylan, Dylan, son of the wave,
The spotted fish now you must save.

Immediately the waters trembled and shook. Huge waves swamped the little boat and it rocked and floundered in the lake.

First one, then two, then three great monstrous fish arose from the water. The first had teeth like harpoons, the second had whiskers taut as the rigging of a ship, and the third had fins as sharp as gaffing hooks.

The three great monstrous fish spent not a moment looking for Dylan. Instead they began to chase the little spotted fish, growling great growls as they swam.

The little spotted fish dashed this way and that, trying to escape.

Dylan looked up the boat and down for a magic rod or net, but there was none. So without a thought more he dove, shirt and trousers and all, into the troubled lake and swam straight towards the little spotted fish.

He scooped up the tiny fish in his hands and swam for shore. All the while the loud growls of the three great monstrous fish were behind him.

Dylan made his way to the shallows where the great monstrous fish could not go. He held the little spotted fish down in the water to keep it cool and wet. Then he turned to look at the three who thrashed angrily off the shore.

Give us back the spotted fish,
And you can have whatever you wish,

growled the three great monsters.

But Dylan only laughed. "I want nothing. I need nothing. And I will not stand idly by while a little one is set upon by three. So take your wishes and a good good-day!"

Without a word more, the three monstrous fish dived below the waves. Their tails slapped so angrily as they went that water spilt out of the lake and rained for miles about.

Then Dylan looked down at the little spotted fish. "Perhaps you should come home with me, little friend," he said. "This lake does not like the looks of us."

At that, the little spotted fish began to tremble and sigh. As Dylan watched, its scales sloughed off like silver leaves in the fall. Its fins peeled away. Its tail dropped off. And before his wondering eyes, the little fish turned into a beautiful girl with silver-gray hair and silver-gray eyes.

"It is well that you came to my aid with your own swimming skill and not with magic," said the girl. "For if you had still owned the rod and net, I would be a little fish yet."

And the girl gave Dylan her hand.

Hand in hand they walked back through the tangled wood to home, where they may be still. For surely they lived a long and happy life, as calm and even as the bones of the herring on either side of the spine.

A Note From the Author About the Story

All tellers of tales draw upon many different experiences, which they change to fit the needs of a particular story. But whereas the old storytellers often had only their own villages and village life to put into their tales, we who make up stories today live in a global village, a village that runs from one end of the world to the other. Through books and magazines, through television and movies, we have learned from more cultures than our great-grandfathers ever knew existed.

So *The Little Spotted Fish* is a combination of a number of things. There is William Butler Yeats' haunting poem, "The Song of Wandering Aengus," and the Irish legend of the spotted trout that leap singing from the mountain streams. There is the Scottish folk wisdom about herrings and the naming of a Welsh princeling in the hero tales, *Mabinogion*. And there is the magic of the number three, which is found in all the occult lore in the world. All those things, and perhaps more I cannot put my finger on at the moment, combined inside me when I sat down to write the story of *The Little Spotted Fish*.

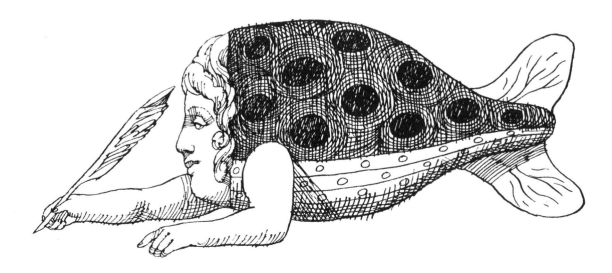